D0688410

Author's Note

The history of the Nutcracker *ballet begins nearly two hundred years ago. The original story, written by E.T.A. Hoffmann, was first published in Germany in 1816 as part of a collection of children's fairy tales. Hoffmann's story of a young girl's adventures with her wooden soldier doll was full of dark and eerie images and quite lengthy. In the mid-1800s, French writer Alexandre Dumas (author of* The Three Musketeers*) reworked Hoffmann's story, making it shorter and sweeter. The* Nutcracker *ballet is based on Dumas's version of the tale.*

A team of talented Russians joined forces in the early 1890s to turn Dumas's Nutcracker *into a ballet. Ivan Vsevolojsky was the director of the Russian Imperial Theatres. He suggested the idea of the ballet to choreographer Marius Petipa and composer Pyotr Ilyich Tchaikovsky. At first neither Petipa nor Tchaikovsky thought the project was worthwhile. But Vsevolojsky finally convinced them to work on it. By April 1892, Tchaikovsky had finished writing the music. In August, Petipa started to work on the dances, but was forced to stop when he became gravely ill. It was his assistant, Lev Ivanov, who completed the choreography. On December 17, 1892,* The Nutcracker *was performed for the first time.*

More than one hundred years later, the ballet is still being performed. Each Christmas season, cities throughout the world stage beautiful and elaborate productions before audiences of all ages. For many families, attending a performance of The Nutcracker *has become a holiday tradition, much like trimming the tree and singing Christmas carols. It is my hope that this book will add to that tradition by giving readers, young and old, a simple version of the classic tale to return to year after year.*

My First Nutcracker

STORY BY E.T.A. HOFFMANN

ADAPTED BY *Stephanie True Peters* ILLUSTRATED BY *Linda Bronson*

Dutton Children's Books

One Christmas Eve long ago, two children peeked through a keyhole to watch their parents trim the tree. At last, the door opened.

"Clara and Fritz, come see!" their mother called.

The tree sparkled from tip to trunk with delicious candy treats. Clara touched a spun-sugar fairy that winked in the candlelight.

Soon after, guests arrived for a grand Christmas party. Merriment filled the house.

Suddenly, an old man wearing a cape as black as raven's wings swept into the room. Children shrank back in fear. But not Clara.

"Godfather Drosselmeyer!" she cried.

The old man lifted her into his arms. Snowmelt kissed her cheeks. "I have something for you." He handed her a wooden toy soldier.

"He's wonderful!" said Clara.

"He's ugly!" said Fritz.

"He's full of surprises," said Godfather Drosselmeyer. He showed the children how the doll could crack nuts between its teeth.

"Let me try!" Fritz yanked the nutcracker from Clara's arms. *Crack!* Its head hit a wall. Its jaw broke in two.

"Oh, no!" Clara cradled her broken toy and wept.

Godfather Drosselmeyer dried Clara's tears with his handkerchief. Then he tied the cloth around the doll's head. "He'll be fine by morning."

The party ended. Parents bundled up their sleepy children and took them home. Clara tucked her nutcracker into a cradle beneath the tree and went to bed.

When the house was still, Godfather Drosselmeyer stole back inside. With gentle fingers, he untied the handkerchief and shook it. Clara's tears turned to shimmering dust and floated from the folds. "At midnight, let the magic begin," he whispered. And he vanished into the night.

As the clock hands inched toward midnight, Clara tiptoed down the stairs. She picked him up and lay beside him on the sofa. "I'll keep you safe," she whispered. She fell asleep just as the first bells chimed.

Shadows stirred. Mice the size of men crept from the corners. Their Mouse King led them on silent feet toward the nutcracker.

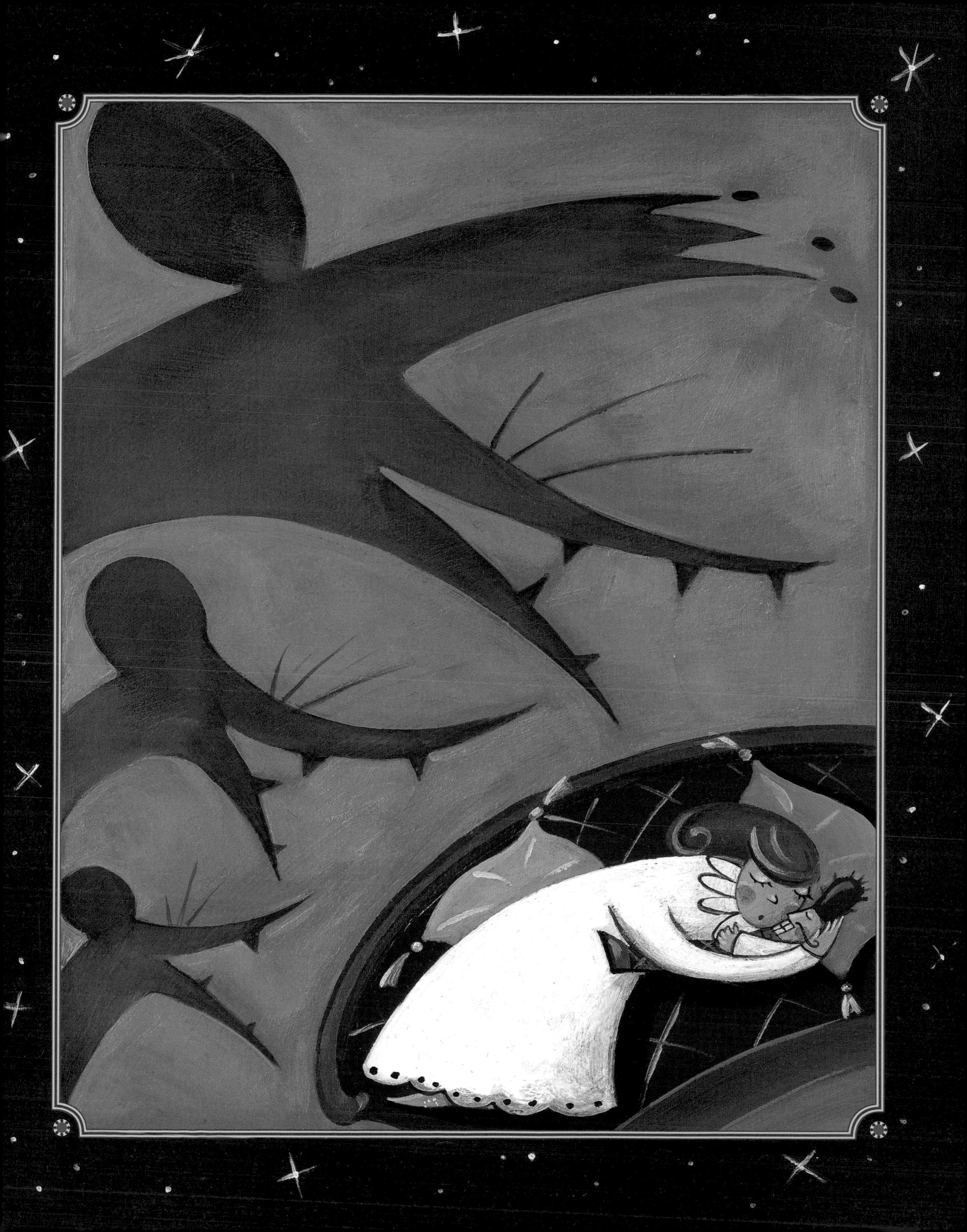

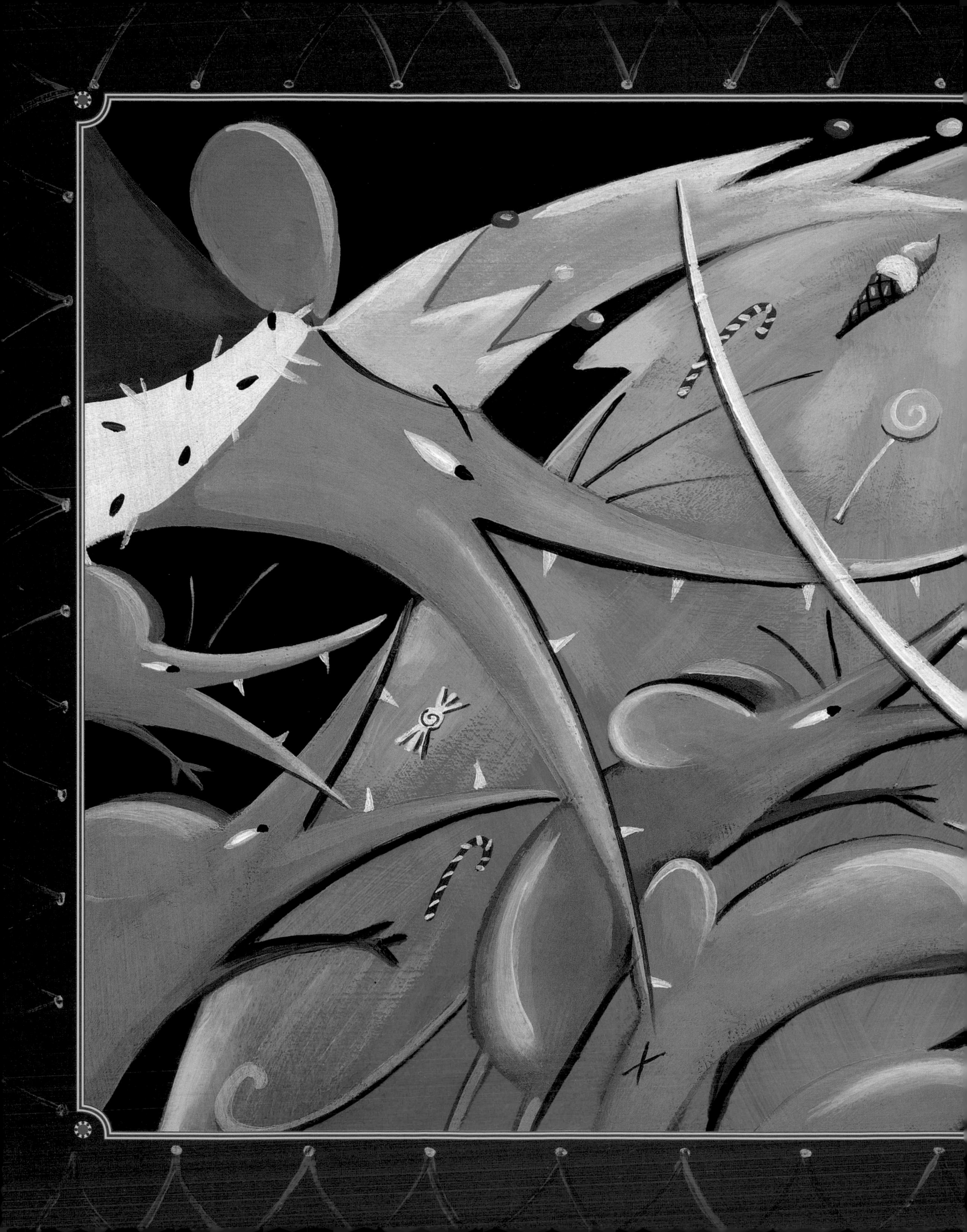

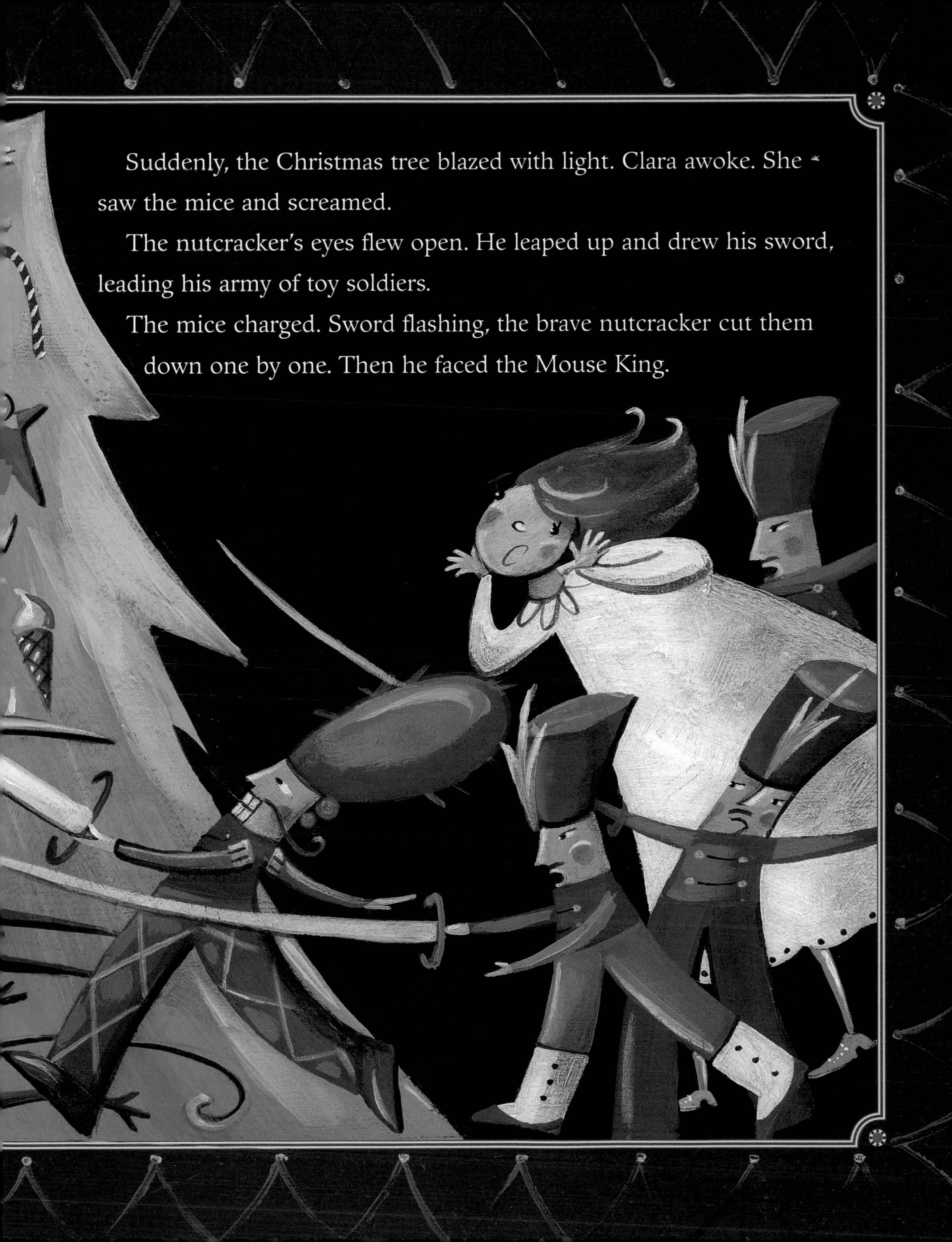

Suddenly, the Christmas tree blazed with light. Clara awoke. She saw the mice and screamed.

The nutcracker's eyes flew open. He leaped up and drew his sword, leading his army of toy soldiers.

The mice charged. Sword flashing, the brave nutcracker cut them down one by one. Then he faced the Mouse King.

The King pounced, grabbing the nutcracker.

"No!" Clara threw her slipper at the King's head. The King dropped the nutcracker. With a mighty thrust, the nutcracker buried his sword into the wicked beast's belly. The King fell to the floor and lay still.

The nutcracker lifted the King's crown high above his head. The air shone with moonlight and magic. Suddenly, a handsome young man stood where the nutcracker had been.

"Who are you?" Clara said.

"I am a prince. The Mouse King imprisoned me in the body of an ugly toy. Your godfather rescued me. Your kindness and bravery broke the evil spell."

He placed the crown on Clara's head. Magic swept over her, changing her nightgown into a dress fit for a princess. At that moment, a gentle voice called to them from outside. "Come!" it beckoned.

Clara and the Prince stepped into the snowy night. A soft breeze swept them up and carried them far, far away . . .

. . . to a magnificent castle. "Welcome," said a beautiful woman in the doorway. "I am the Sugar Plum Fairy."

Clara stared. It was the fairy from her tree. And around her were all the other candy decorations come to life!

The Fairy smiled. "We saw how you saved our prince. Come in, and let us dance for you."

Clara sat beside the Prince on a marshmallow throne. Musicians struck up a melody that set her toes tapping.

The first dancer, Chocolate, whirled onto the stage. He spun round, faster and faster, until he seemed to melt into a rich brown puddle. Then sweet Coffee floated in on a sea of frothy lace. Chinese Tea followed, bobbing deep bows.

Next, snappy red-and-white peppermints tumbled and leaped like puppies at play. Finally, Mother Ginger hurried in—and out popped her children from beneath her billowing skirt!

The music turned as gentle as a lullaby.

The Sugar Plum Fairy led the Nutcracker Prince to the floor. Together they danced a dreamy duet. Clara's heart soared.

The Prince returned to Clara's side. "Daylight is near. It's time to go." They climbed into a crystal sleigh piled high with pillows. As they soared into the air, Clara fell fast asleep.

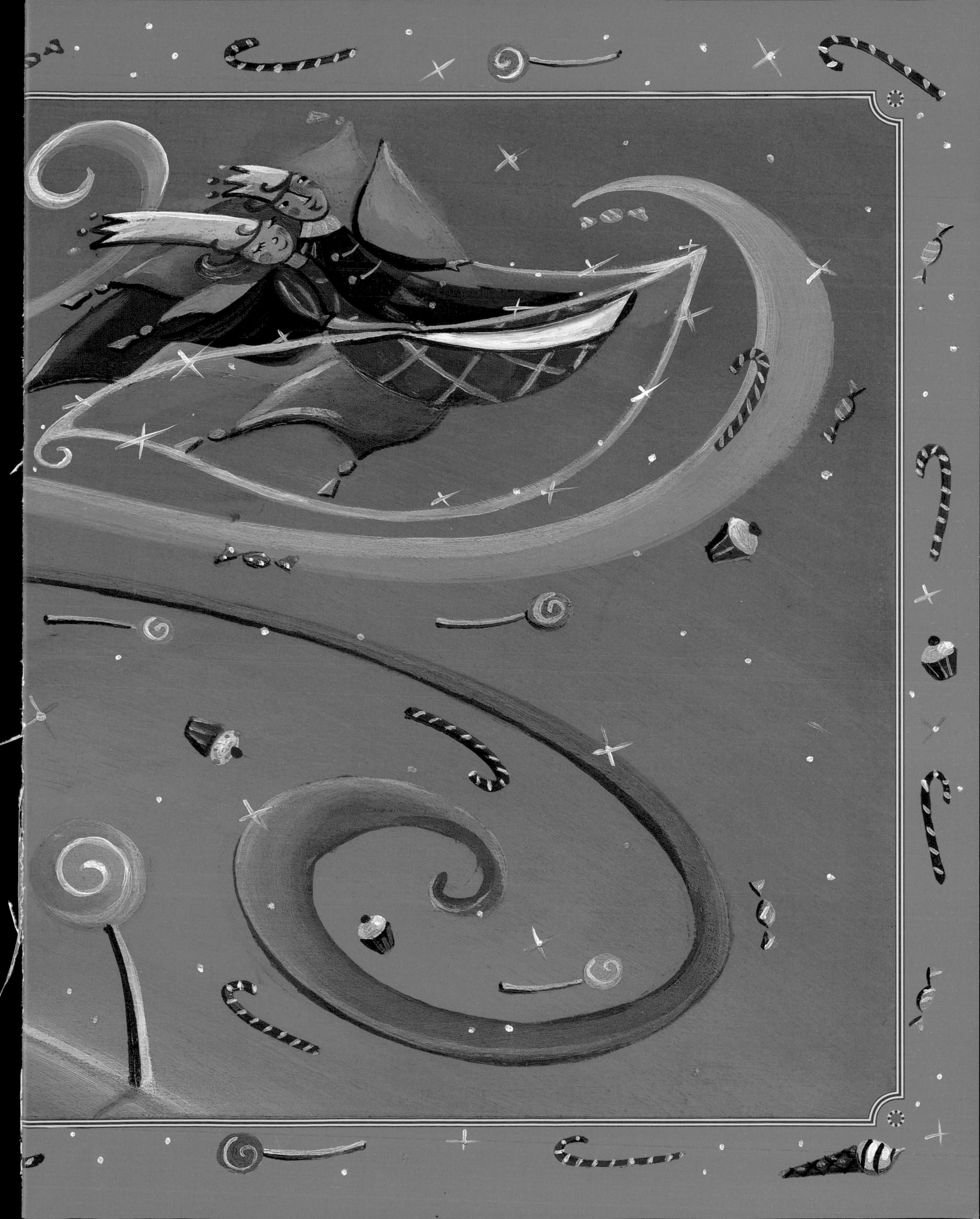

Sunlight warmed Clara's cheek. She awoke to find that her handsome prince was once again an ugly nutcracker. But his jaw was no longer broken. And on her head, she found a crown.

For Dan, Jackson, and Chloe

~S.T.P.

To my darling daughter, Frances, with love

~L.B.

DUTTON CHILDREN'S BOOKS A division of Penguin Young Readers Group
Published by the Penguin Group • Penguin Group (USA) Inc., 375 Hudson Street, New York, New York 10014, U.S.A.
Penguin Group (Canada), 90 Eglinton Avenue East, Suite 700, Toronto, Ontario, Canada M4P 2Y3 (a division of Pearson Penguin Canada Inc.) • Penguin Books Ltd, 80 Strand, London WC2R 0RL, England • Penguin Ireland, 25 St Stephen's Green, Dublin 2, Ireland (a division of Penguin Books Ltd) • Penguin Group (Australia), 250 Camberwell Road, Camberwell, Victoria 3124, Australia (a division of Pearson Australia Group Pty Ltd) • Penguin Books India Pvt Ltd, 11 Community Centre, Panchsheel Park, New Delhi - 110 017, India • Penguin Group (NZ), 67 Apollo Drive, Mairangi Bay, Auckland 1311, New Zealand (a division of Pearson New Zealand Ltd) • Penguin Books (South Africa) (Pty) Ltd, 24 Sturdee Avenue, Rosebank, Johannesburg 2196, South Africa
Penguin Books Ltd, Registered Offices: 80 Strand, London WC2R 0RL, England

CIP Data is available.

Published in the United States by Dutton Children's Books, a division of Penguin Young Readers Group
345 Hudson Street, New York, New York 10014 www.penguin.com/youngreaders

Designed by Irene Vandervoort
Manufactured in China First Edition
ISBN 978-0-525-47687-0
1 3 5 7 9 10 8 6 4 2